Beamer Visits
The Emergency Room

The Beamer Book Series

Written by Cindy Chambers and Tina Demme

Illustrated by Jim Huber

Beamer Visits The Emergency Room and all associated illustrations are

copyright 2015 The Tell Me Town Foundation

All Rights Reserved.

Beamer Visits The Emergency Room
Second Release

No part of this publication may be reproduced, stored in a retrieval system, or transmitted,
in any form or by any means, electronic, mechanical, photocopying, recording,
or otherwise, without the written permission of the author.

First published by Dog Ear Publishing
4010 W. 86th Street, Ste H
Indianapolis, IN 46268
www.dogearpublishing.net

ISBN: 978-1-4575-1289-6

This book is printed on acid-free paper.

This book is a work of fiction. Places, events, and situations in this book are purely fictional
and any resemblance to actual persons, living or dead, is coincidental.

Printed in the United States of America

Our Special Thanks

To Dr. Edward Puccio, MD, FACEP for his compassionate commitment to health care excellence and his kindness toward children and animals

To The Inova Health System

To Inova Loudoun Hospital's doctors, nurses and staff members for their outstanding dedication to compassionate care

To the staff and board members of the Inova Loudoun Hospital Foundation for their tireless dedication and commitment to those in need

To Samantha Leahy for showing us the tender kindness of the Child Life Specialist

To Jim Huber for illustrating this meanigful story

To Jay and Serena Huber for their wonderful color suggestions and for making dad proud

To Kyle Mitchell for being a wonderful example of kindness and compassion

To Elizabeth Dotur for her professional editing and advice

To Cathy Christopher, Anne Blackstone and the rest of the staff of Inova Loudoun Hospital Rehabilitation Center for their commitment to helping others

To Amber and Kyle Sparling for their commitment and bravery

To our family members for their love, encouragement and belief in our dreams for this book and "The Beamer Series"

To Harriet Mayor Fulbright for her friendship and her belief in quality education for all

To Gokhan Coskun for his dedication to education and his positive outlook on life

To the Brown family for their wonderful support to all children in need

To Debbie Rieger for her friendship and support throughout this project

To Kimberly Ruff for her kindness and advice early in this journey

To Gina, Max, Sammie, Stephie, Lucy, CoCo, Libby, Pepper, Furbert, Tyler, Blanca, Dugan, Don, Snowball, Persephone, Bandit, Camille, Sophie, Shadow, Leia, Boss and all the other animals in the world we love so much

Dedication

This book is dedicated to Macari Brown and all of the special children of the world whose beautiful spirits and bravery deserve our unconditional love and support.

Macari Can Write His Name Now!

The above was hand written by Macari Brown at age 5 through his strength, bravery and determination to be the very best that he can be.

Hi, my name is Beamer.

I am four years old. I live in Tell Me Town. I am a therapy dog. That means I help people feel better just by being around and letting them pet me.

One day I was visiting the emergency room at the hospital. I noticed a little boy crying when his sister quickly asked, "Beamer, can you come help my brother Max feel better?"

I knew I could help him feel better. So I asked Max, "What's wrong?"

He replied, "I hurt my leg and my mom brought me here. I don't know what's going to happen, and I'm scared."

I told Max I could help him understand what would happen in the emergency room by telling him a story about what happened to me when I was a puppy.

Max was very interested, so I started my story.

He listened carefully.

When I was a puppy, Kyle was my very best friend. We always played ball together. Everyday we would run and play. It was so much fun.

One day Kyle and I were outside running in the yard playing ball when it started to rain. We were having so much fun; we kept playing anyway. That's when I slipped on the wet grass and hurt my leg.

Kyle picked me up and took me home. "Mom, Dad," he cried, "Beamer hurt his leg! What should we do?"

Right away Kyle's mom said, "We should take Beamer to the emergency room. The nice people there will know how to help him."

As he held me gently, Kyle looked at his mom and said, "Okay mom, I love Beamer very much and I want him to get help right away."

So off we went to the emergency room.

When we got to the emergency room, Kyle hugged me gently as he carried me inside. I started to cry because I was scared, so Kyle held me close and said, "Don't worry Beamer, everything will be alright."

Before I knew it, a nice lady, who said she was a nurse, told us it was my turn to go with her. She said Kyle could go too. I was so glad.

She put a colored band on my leg and Kyle got one just like it for his arm. She said the band meant Kyle and I belonged together.

The nurse brought us to a room with a bed. Kyle put me on the bed so the nurse could see my leg better. Then Kyle told her how I got hurt. She was very nice to me.

Next, a happy lady came by and said, "Hi Beamer, I'm Sammie. I will be 'Beamer's Buddy' and stay with you the whole time you are here." Her badge read *Child Life Specialist*.

Then Sammie smiled at me, and rubbed my head.
I liked her right away.

Sammie told me another nice person called a technician would come in to check and see if everything else about me was okay.

Sammie told me that nothing the technician was going to do would hurt me. She was right, it didn't hurt at all!

Sammie told me the other person who would come to see me would be Dr. Poochio. She told me that children and animals love Dr. Poochio because he is so gentle and nice.

I asked Sammie if anything the doctor was going to do would hurt me.

She said Dr. Poochio would never want to hurt me. She said she would tell him about my leg and he would be extra careful with it.

When Dr. Poochio came in, he smiled and said,
"Hello Beamer, I'm Dr. Poochio."

I could tell he really liked puppies. He told me I
was a good puppy and he was happy to meet me. He
made me smile.

Then, Dr. Poochio said he was going to look at my leg to see what he could do to help make it better. He promised to be very gentle with me. Then he gave me a pat on the head.

Next, Dr. Poochio said he needed to take an X-ray of my leg. He said an X-ray is a special picture that he would look at to see if my leg was okay. He said it wouldn't hurt.

Kyle carried me into the X-ray room. Dr. Poochio was right! The X-ray didn't hurt.

Dr. Poochio looked at the X-ray and said, "You have a sprained leg. That means the muscle just got pulled a little, but nothing is broken."

He said,
"Beamer, you'll be feeling better very soon."

So, Dr. Poochio wrapped my leg up in a bandage to make it comfortable and help it heal.

Then he gave me a hug and said good-bye. He told me that I was a brave puppy and that he was very proud of me.

Then Sammie gave me a gentle hug and said good-bye. I thanked her for being so nice and staying with me the whole time. I told her that I would really miss her.

She said she would always be
"Beamer's Buddy."

When Kyle's mom and dad saw us, they were so happy to see that I was already feeling better.

As we left, I waved good-bye to all my new friends in the emergency room.

I liked the people at the hospital so much. I wanted to go and find some other hurt animals and take them to the emergency room so they could feel better too!

"Okay Beamer," said Max. "Now that I've heard your story, I see that I don't need to be afraid. The nice people in the emergency room are my friends, just like you. They care about me and want to help me feel better."

I put my head on Max's knee and said, "I'll sit here with you Max, and we'll wait for your turn to see Dr. Poochio."

Max smiled, put his arm around me and said, "Now I'm Beamer's Buddy, too."

I gently leaned against Max and said, "Yes Max, and you always will be."

Beamer's "real life" Emergency Room Buddies

Dr. Edward Puccio, MD, FACEP (Dr. Poochio)

Dr. Puccio is the Medical Director for the Emergency Department at Inova Loudoun Hospital in Leesburg, Virginia. Dr. Puccio did his emergency residency at Allegheny General Hospital in Pennsylvania. He did his internship and residency in General Surgery at Georgetown University Hospital in Washington D.C. Dr. Puccio graduated from The University of Pittsburgh School of Medicine where he received his MD. He attended Duke University in Durham, NC where he received a Bachelor of Science Degree in Zoology.

Samantha Leahy (Sammie)

Samantha is a certified Child Life Specialist. She received her Master's in Applied Development Psychology from George Mason University, her Bachelor's Degree in Psychology from the University of Central Florida, and her certification in Child Life from the National Child Life Council. Samantha works with children and their families in Pediatric Emergency Services at Inova Loudoun Hospital in Leesburg, Virginia.

Kyle Mitchell (Kyle)

Kyle lives in Maryland with his family. Along with studying and playing football and lacrosse, Kyle dedicates his time to helping others in need. Kyle is a recipient of the 2012 Excalibur Award from Inova Loudoun Hospital for his commitment to helping those in need; especially children.

About the Authors:

Cindy Chambers was raised in a large family filled with lots of laughter, children and pets. She has enjoyed writing since she was a child. Cindy has been instrumental in raising hundreds of thousands of dollars for charities. Because of her strong interest in education, health, writing, and helping others, she created *The Beamer Book Series*™, Tell Me Town Books™, and The Tell Me Town Foundation. Cindy has received awards and recognition for her commitment to helping others, and for Tell Me Town and *The Beamer Book Series*. The author and the series have appeared in news and magazine articles, and on television news.

Tina Demme lives in Maryland and has three beautiful dogs, and a cat. Because of her love for animals, she volunteers in her community, helping dogs in need, find new and loving homes. She promotes responsible pet ownership, rescue and adoption. Tina is also a loving mom who supports healthcare charities and various organizations that support the animal-human connection.

Cindy and Tina wrote *Beamer Visits The Emergency Room* because of their love and compassion for children and animals. They wanted to reduce the fear and mystery of going to the emergency room, and at the same time, introduce some of the wonderful people that make the experience as comforting as possible for children.

About The Tell Me Town Foundation

The Tell Me Town Foundation, is a 501(c) (3) public charity, established to provide comfort and education to children and their families as they learn about life, health and safety. Through The Beamer Book Series, Tell Me Town Books, and the Tell Me Town website, children and their families learn about these important topics, in a delightful setting where everyone is treated with kindness and respect.

To find out more about Tell Me Town and **The Beamer Book Series** please visit us at www.tellmetown.com.

"Like" Tell Me Town on Facebook and follow us on Twitter

CPSIA information can be obtained
at www.ICGtesting.com
Printed in the USA
BVHW020429200419
546043BV00001B/1/P